For the baby
I love:

Baby's Book of Winnie the Pooh

A Disney Treasury of Stories and Songs for Baby

Disney PRESS

NEW YORK

Contents

Introduction...6

Baby-Play Rhymes.............................9

Pooh's Honey Tree............................21

Pooh's Friends................................47

Find a Friend.................................53

A to Zzzz....................................65

Numbers.....................................97

Colors.......................................105

Shapes 113

Opposites....................................123

Senses.......................................135

Feelings 143

Pooh's Day...................................151

Pooh Gets Stuck..............................159

Bedtime Hummables...........................177

Introduction

Dear Parents and Caregivers:

It's never too early to begin reading to your child. And we at Disney believe that it is never too early to introduce your infant son or daughter to the lovable, huggable Pooh and his friends, Tigger, Eeyore, Piglet, Rabbit, Kanga, and Roo. You'll meet them all in *Baby's Book of Winnie the Pooh*. This lovely anthology is full of verses, stories, and activities that you and your child, at different ages and stages, can visit over and over again.

Let's begin with infants, from newborn to three months. The rhythms and rhymes in this book are pleasant to hear, and just the right length for little ears. Read some of them to your infant as you hold her close. She'll enjoy the sounds, patterns, and rhythms. As she grows, she'll learn to mimic those sounds and pick up the movements—touching toes, bouncing, and clapping. These playful games keep your child attentive, and help develop eye-hand coordination and the other small motor skills. And of course bring lots of giggly fun!

An activity you can enjoy with your six- to nine-month-old is looking at the pictures and turning the pages together. Your child may only be seeing colors and shapes early on, but later will recognize what is happening in a picture and be able to point to specific objects when you ask. Book content begins to take on a little more meaning.

Your toddler (ages one to three) will enjoy revisiting these verses, and with confidence, demonstrate for you how much she has remembered. Your toddler will also enjoy talking about the pictures

depicting Pooh trying to get Piglet to sleep, the whole group taking a bath, and Tigger jumping on the bed. Your child will no doubt relate to all these bedtime rituals and behaviors. They're so universal! And certainly they can serve as prompts for discussion. "Do *you* wear a nightcap to bed?" "What are your favorite jammies?" "What do you play with in the tub?" "What story shall we read tonight?"

With the "Find a Friend" section of this anthology, you can help your child develop visual awareness. Ask him to point to Owl, both on the left page and then on the right. Where is he? Where is Kanga? If your three-year-old is ready to learn some words, you can point, for example, to the picture of Pooh, and have your child "read" the name *Pooh* printed below the character.

After enjoying the lively hums of "A to Zzzz," you may want to recite (or sing) the alphabet together. At different times, explore other beginning concepts together. Read and talk about numbers at one sitting; colors, shapes, or opposites at other times. As attention spans lengthen with age, your child will enjoy hearing you read aloud the stories about Pooh and his adventures with honey.

No matter what age or what stage your child is at, *Baby's Book of Winnie the Pooh* has enough material for many hours, days, weeks, and years of pleasurable reading for you to share. Have fun together!

Sincerely,
The Editors

Baby-Play Rhymes

Round and round the garden like a teddy bear, ONE step, TWO steps, Tickle you under there! •

Tap fingers along Baby's body; end with a tickle.

A toe-tickling rhyme, from big toe to little.

This little piggy went to market,
and this little piggy stayed home;
This little piggy had roast beef,
and this little piggy had none:
And this little piggy cried

"Wee, wee, wee," all the way home.

Open, shut them.

(On "open," hold your hands open wide.
On "shut," ball hands into fists.)

Open, shut them.

Give a little clap.

(Clap hands.)

Open, shut them.

Put them in your lap.

(Fold hands in lap.)

Creep them, creep them

(Starting at Baby's tummy, move fingers
toward Baby's face.)

Slowly creep them

Right up to your chin.

(Gently pull Baby's chin downward.)

Open up your mouth

(Gently pull Baby's mouth.)

But do not let them in.

(Run your fingers back down Baby's body toward tummy.)

This is a hand-patting rhyme. Trace the letter B on Baby's palm.

Pat-a-cake, pat-a-cake,
baker's man,
Bake me a cake as fast as you can.
Pat it and
roll it and
mark it with a **B,**
And put it in the oven for Baby and me.

A tickle game, from
Baby's toes to nose.

Baby Bye, butterfly
We must watch him
You and I.
There he goes
On his toes,
Over Baby's nose.

(Hold Baby above you,)

Dance to your daddy,

My little baby,

Dance to your daddy,

My little lamb!

(then pull close.)

You shall have a fishy

In a little dishy,

You shall have a fishy

When the boat comes in.

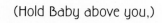

(Hold Baby above you,)

Dance to your daddy,

My little baby,

Dance to your daddy,

My little lamb;

(then pull close.)

You shall have an apple,

You shall have a plum,

You shall have a rattle-basket,

When your dad comes home.

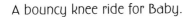

A bouncy knee ride for Baby.

This is the way the ladies ride,

Nimble-nim, nimble-nim;

This is the way the gentlemen ride,

Gallop-a-trot! Gallop-a-trot!

This is the way the farmer rides,

Jiggety-jog, jiggety-jog;

This is the way the butcher boy rides,

Trippety-trot, trippety-trot,

Till he falls in a ditch with a flipperty,

Flipperty, flop, flop, FLOP!

Rock-a-bye, Baby, in the treetop,

When the wind blows, the cradle will rock.

When the bough breaks, the cradle will fall,

And down will come baby, cradle, and all.

Shh . . .

I'll buy you a tartan bonnet,
And feathers to put upon it,
With a hush-a-bye and a lullaby,
Because you are so like your daddy.

Sweet dreams, Baby.

Shoe a little horse,
Shoe a little mare,
But let the little colt
Go bare, bare, bare.

Bounce Baby on your knee.

Derry, down derry, and up in the air,

Baby shall ride without pony or mare,

Clasped in my arms like a queen on a throne,

Prettiest rider that ever was known.

Swing Baby up and down, end rhyme with Baby hugged close.

A finger-touching game, from thumb to pinky.

This is mama, kind and dear.

This is papa, standing near.

This is brother, see how tall!

This is sister, not so tall.

This is baby, sweet and small.

These are the family one and all!

End with wiggling all of Baby's fingers.

Clap, clap handies,
Mommy's wee, wee one;
Clap, clap handies,
Daddy's coming home;
Home to his bonny
Wee bit baby;
Clap, clap handies,
My wee, wee one.

Clap Baby's hands together.

Twinkle, twinkle, little star.

How I wonder what you are.

Up above the world so high,

Like a diamond in the sky.

Twinkle, twinkle, little star.

How I wonder what you are.

Shh . . .

Pooh's
Honey Tree

Winnie the Pooh had a big, round tummy.
Pooh's tummy was always quite hungry.

Hungry for honey!

"Oh bother!" said Pooh, looking in his honeypot. Empty.

Just then, Pooh heard a sound.

BUZZ! BUZZ! BUZZ!

Something small and fuzzy flew past his ear.
BUZZ! BUZZ! BUZZ!

"Oh!" said Pooh. "A bee!"

Pooh followed the bee.
Soon they came to
a honey tree!

Up the tree Pooh went. Up. Up. Up.

Then, *CRACK!* A branch broke.
Down the tree Pooh fell.
Down.
Down.
Down.

Pooh rubbed his sore head.

Pooh needed help.

He went to
Christopher Robin's
house. He saw that
his friend had a
big blue balloon.

"May I borrow your balloon?" Pooh asked.

"Here, Pooh," said Christopher Robin, giving him the balloon.

"Thank you," said Pooh. "I'm going to use this balloon to float up to a honey tree."

"Silly old bear," said Christopher Robin. "The bees will not let you near their honey."

At that, Pooh sat down in the mud and rolled around.

"Look!" said Pooh. "The bees will think I'm a little black rain cloud. They will not even know I am there."

Christopher Robin sat down to see
what would happen next.

Pooh held on to the balloon. He floated up
to the top of the honey tree.

Pooh reached into the bees' nest and pulled out a pawful of golden honey.

BUZZ! BUZZ! BUZZ! The bees did not think that Pooh was a little black rain cloud. They thought he was a hungry bear!

Suddenly, the balloon string came undone, and the air swooshed out!

Pooh and his balloon sailed over the treetops.

Finally the balloon lost
all its air. Down it came.
And down came Pooh.

Pooh landed right in Christopher Robin's arms!
Pooh looked up at the bees in the tree. Then he
looked at Christopher Robin. "Oh dear!" Pooh said.
"I guess it all comes from liking honey so much!"

Pooh's
Friends

The most wonderful
thing about
Piglets
is Piglets are
huggable things.

The most wonderful
thing about
Tiggers
is Tiggers are made out of springs.

The most wonderful
thing about
Eeyores
is the way they
make life sunny.

The most wonderful
thing about
Rabbits
is their pantries are
filled up with honey.

The most wonderful
thing about
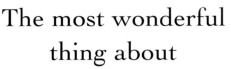
is the time they
share with Roo.

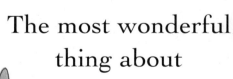

The most wonderful
thing about
Roos
is the generous
things that they do.

The most wonderful
thing about
Owls
is the stories they
tell every day.

The most wonderful
thing about
friends
is the love they
bring our way!

Find
a
Friend

Pooh and all of his friends
pictured below appear in
the scene on the next page.
Point to all the matches.

Pooh

Roo

Kanga

Tigger

Piglet

Owl

Rabbit

Eeyore

Birdhouse

Lettuce

Water Pail

Seed packets

Wheelbarrow

RABBIT'S LIST
PEARS
APPLES
CORN

Corn

Boat

Bush

Beehive

Cattails

Shoes

Stump

Kite

Honey Pot

Bowl

Mailbox

Balloon

Door

Cookies

Castle

Toy Chest

Book

Balls

Bed

Pictures

Blocks

Bat

Aa Bb

Cc Dd

A to Zzzz

A IS FOR ACORN

From atop an oak tree
In the Hundred-Acre Wood
A little acorn fell
Right where Pooh Bear stood.

B IS FOR BEARS

Some bears growl,
some bears snort.
But Pooh Bear is the
humming sort.

C IS FOR CARROTS

Carrots are so
Good to munch,
Rabbit grows them
By the bunch.

D

IS

FOR

DOOR

In spring, Pooh's door
Is open wide
To let the sunshine
Come inside.

E IS FOR EEYORE

Eeyore's gray.
Although it's true,
He's frequently
A little blue.

F IS FOR FOOTPRINTS

Our footprints always follow us
On days when it's been snowing.
They always show us
   where we've been,
But never where we're going.

G IS FOR GOPHER

"Hello!" says Gopher
    to Winnie the Pooh.
"I've just come up
    To visit with you!"

H IS FOR HONEY

"My favorite snack,"
    Says Winnie the Pooh.
"Is one jar of honey . . .
    Or possibly two!"

Ee Ff Gg Hh Ii Jj Kk Ll Mm

I

IS
FOR
ICE SKATES

Though others give
Him funny glances,
On ice skates Pooh Bear
Takes no chances.

Rr Ss Tt Uu

J IS FOR JUMP

Rum-tee-tiddle-tum
Tiddle-tum-too,
When Kanga jumps,
So does Roo.

K IS FOR KITE

When the blustery
Autumn breezes blow,
Up in the air
Kite and Piglet go!

L IS FOR LADDER

A ladder is helpful
Going up and down trees.
When hunting for honey
Or running from bees.

M IS FOR MIRROR

"The Pooh in the mirror is
Quite clever," says Pooh.
"He knows how to copy
Whatever I do."

N IS FOR NOSE

Why have we,
Do you suppose,
Two eyes, two ears,
But just one nose?

O IS FOR OWL

Owl likes to talk a lot.
He's really quite a bore!
He tells Pooh everything he knows.
And sometimes even more!

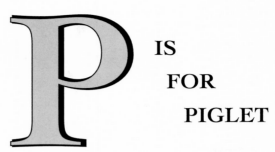

P IS FOR PIGLET

Piglet is so
Very small.
Sometimes
He can't be
Seen at all!

Q

IS
FOR
QUILT

Let it snow and
Let it storm!
Under his quilt
Pooh is cozy and warm!

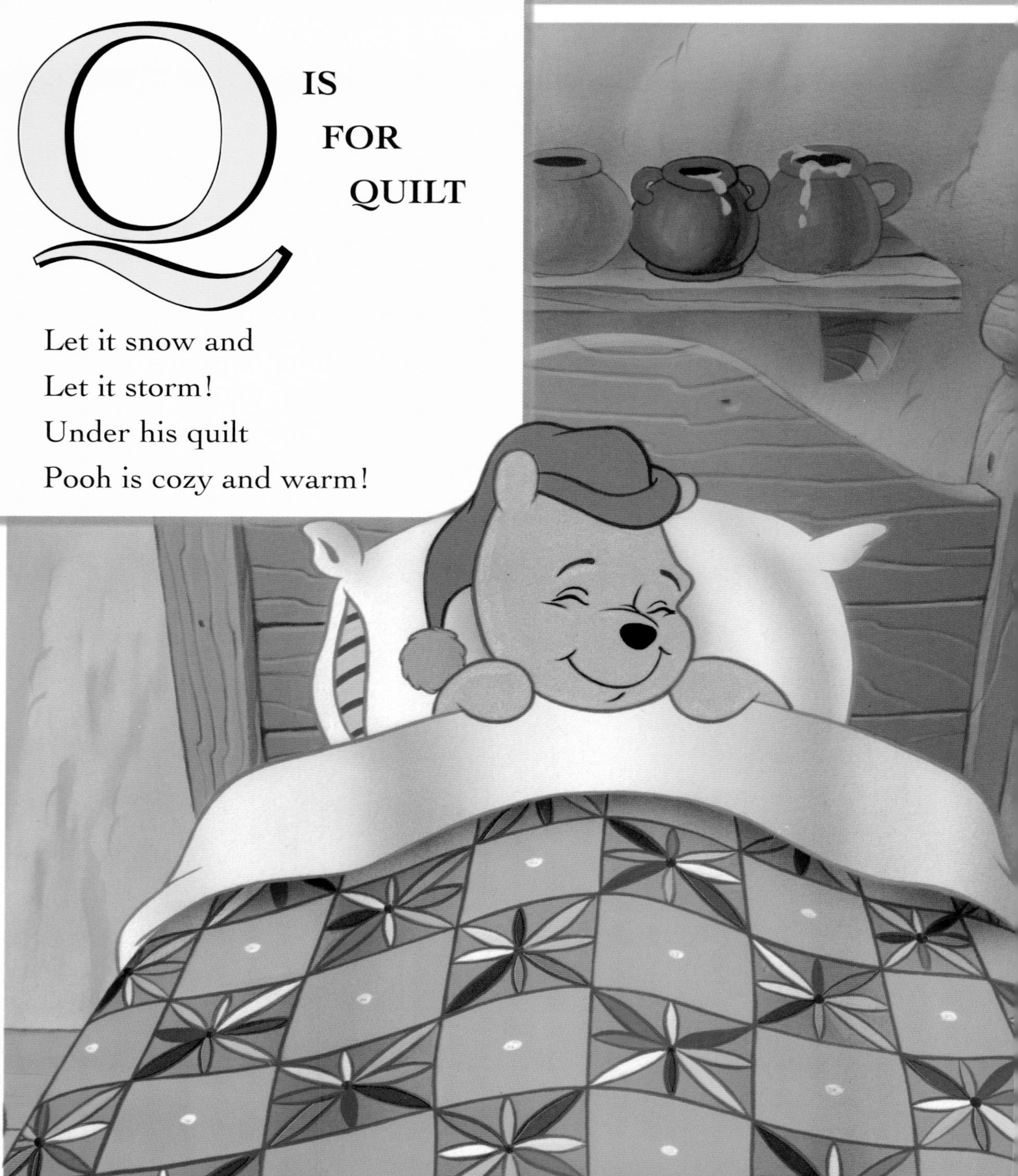

R IS FOR RABBIT

Rabbit is so
Very busy.
Watching him
Makes Pooh Bear dizzy.

Aa Bb Cc Dd

S IS FOR SEESAW

Never make
A seesaw date
With a bear
Who's overweight!

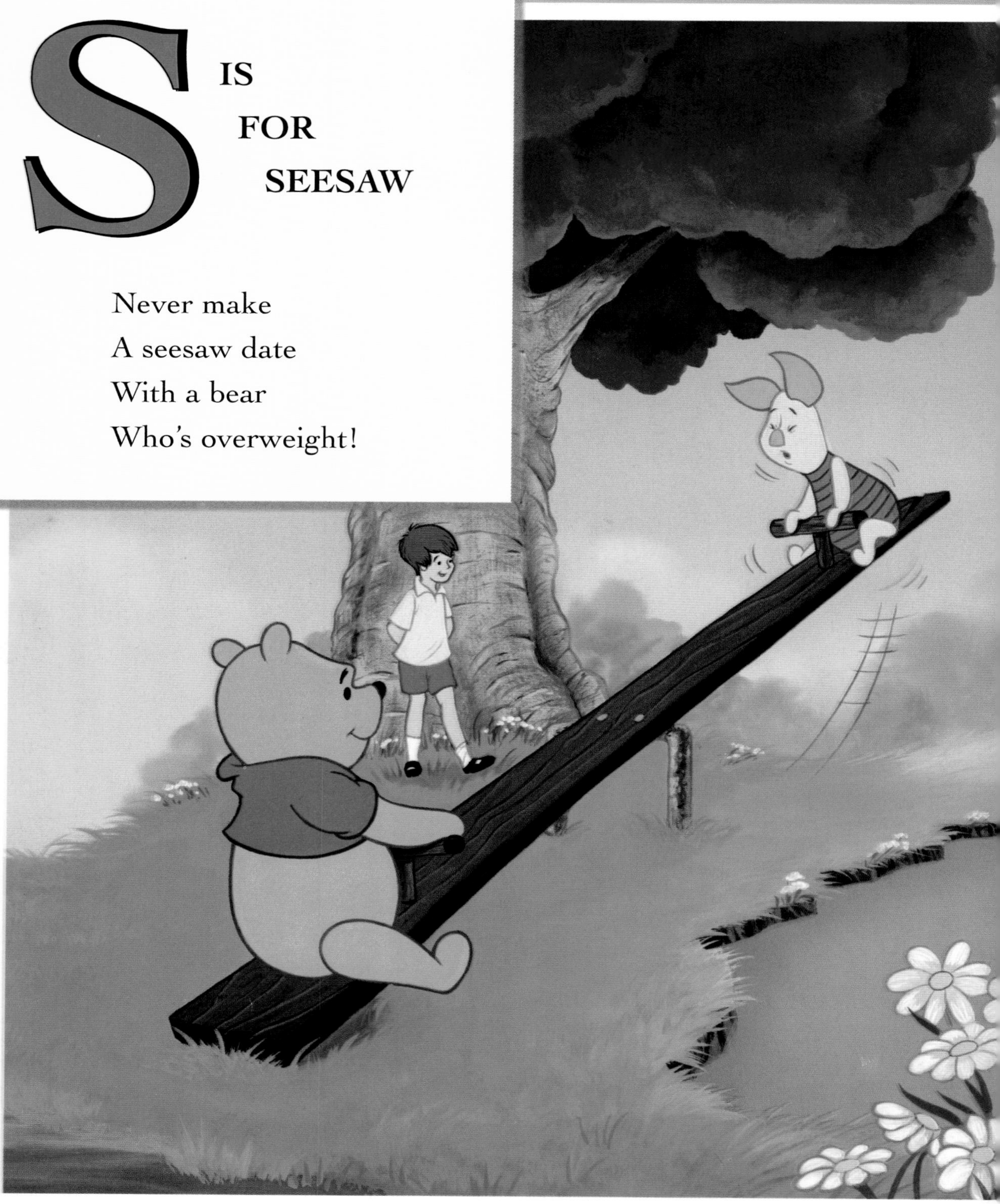

Nn Oo Pp Qq

Vv Ww Xx Yy Zz

Ee Ff Gg Hh Ii Jj Kk Ll Mm

T IS FOR TIGGER

Though winter's here
And birds don't sing,
Tigger's tail still
Has its spring!

Rr Ss Tt Uu

U IS FOR UMBRELLA

Clever Pooh
Is now afloat
In his own
Umbrella boat!

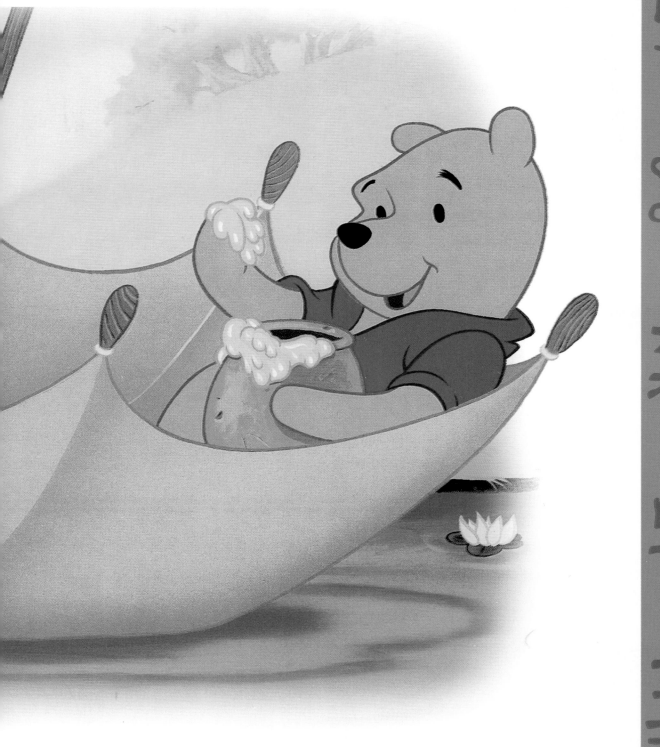

V IS FOR VEST

Piglet's vest
Is warm and snug.
It fits him like
An all-day hug!

W IS FOR WOOZLE

There's nothing to fear
From a woozle it seems.
They're only found
In Pooh Bear's dreams.

X IS FOR XYLOPHONE

Pooh's made a honeypot
Xylophone,
And, oh, it has the
Sweetest tone.

Y IS FOR YAWN

Put on your nightcap,
You old sleepyhead!
A yawn is what your face does
To say, "It's time for bed!"

Z IS FOR ZZZZ

A sound that Pooh
Makes frequently
Begins and ends
With the letter Z.

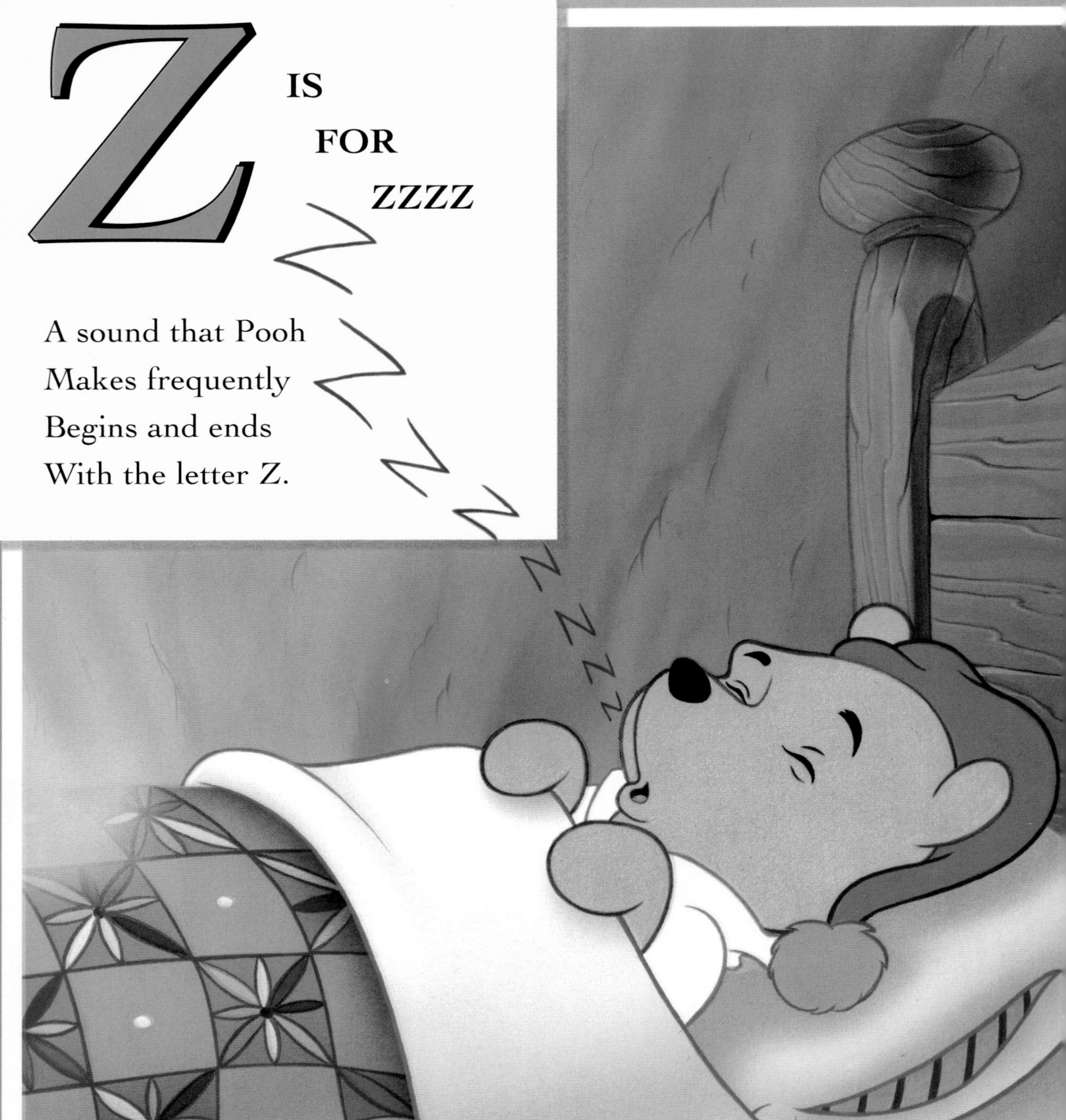

Aa Bb Cc Dd

Zz Yy Xx Ww Vv

Nn Oo Pp Qq

Ee Ff Gg Hh

A B C D E

F G H I J K

L M N O P

Q R S T U

V W X Y Z

Ii Jj Kk Ll Mm

Rr Ss Tt Uu

Numbers

1 One
happy
butterfly
dancing in
the sky.

2 Two great big acorns
to make an acorn pie.

3 Three

pots of honey
will make
a special
treat.

4 Four

bags of carrots
for all the
friends
to eat.

5 Five giant bouncing balls, lined up in a row

6 Six

pretty yellow kites
with orange tails
in tow.

7
Seven
purple flowers
in a little
spotted
vase.

8
Eight
books of stories—
just in case.

9
Nine

red and blue balloons.
Hip, hip, hooray!

10 Ten friends to celebrate a Hundred-Acre day.

Colors

Five little honeypots all in a line,

Pooh reached for the  yellow one and said, "It's dinnertime!"

Four little honeypots all full of honey,

Pooh picked up the
red
pot next.
Look at Pooh's big
tummy!

Three little honeypots all in a row,

Pooh reached for the purple pot.
Two more pots to go.

Two little honeypots, one green, the other blue,

Pooh took down the green pot
and emptied that one, too.

One little honeypot alone up on the shelf,

"Oh dear!" said hungry Pooh.
"The blue pot's by itself!"

Yellow, red, purple, green, blue!

Five little honeypots, sitting on the floor.
"Mmmm!" Pooh said happily.
"I wish I had some more!"

Shapes

oval

triangle

circle

square

There's a party today for Winnie the Pooh!
Let's tag along and learn shapes, too.

Tigger's bouncy, bouncing ball
flies through the air—now watch it fall!

square

Eeyore's gift is bright and blue.
These blocks will be a treat for Pooh.

rectangle

Rabbit is a practical friend—
"A tea towel is the gift to send."

diamond

Owl wisely brings a kite.
"Now, don't forget to hold on tight!"

triangle

The bright new sail sways and swings
on the present Christopher Robin brings.

The heart-shaped card addressed to Pooh
is signed with love from little Roo.

heart

oval

Piglet has the perfect present—
"This pink balloon is very pleasant."

star

Just as his birthday is almost gone,
Pooh spots a star for wishing on.
But he tells his pals, "With friends like you,
All my wishes have come true."

Opposites

up

down

Piglet is small,
truly tiny to see.

Tigger is big,
just as big as can be.

Tigger bounces *high* over puddles below.

Pooh waves to him from a spot way down *low*.

If he's out in the rain,
poor Eeyore gets
wet.

Roo stays dry
because his mom is all set!

Pooh Bear loves honey
because it's
smooth
and sweet.

Eeyore likes thistles—they're
prickly
to eat.

Piglet loves  **Sunny** days because there's so much to do.

Pooh Bear knows **cloudy** ones are lots of fun, too!

Sometimes Eeyore
feels a little bit
sad,

but Pooh Bear
is happy because
you make him
glad.

Tigger jumps
over
whatever's
around.

Rabbit spends
hours deep
under
the ground.

Owl flies far in a sky so blue,

but Pooh Bear
stays
near
to be close to you!

All of the friends are **different**, you see,

but they share the **same** love,
and that is the key.

Senses

hearing

touch

smell

sight

taste

Sight

Winnie the Pooh has two round eyes.

Pooh *sees* with his eyes.

Yellow and black, fuzzy and fast —
he *sees* a honeybee.

Hearing

Pooh has two
soft ears.

Pooh *hears* with his ears.

Buzz!
Buzz!

He *hears*
the honeybee.

Smell

Pooh has one nose—right in the middle of his face.

Pooh *smells* with his nose.

Sniff, sniff!

He *smells* his favorite snack.

Touch

Pooh has two
fuzzy paws.

Pooh touches with his paws.

Pooh touches
the honey tree.
The tree feels
bumpy and
rough.

Taste

Pooh has one pink tongue.
He **tastes** with
his tongue.

Mmm!

Pooh **tastes** yummy honey!

Feelings

Hee-hee-hee!

When Pooh is with his friends,
he feels cheerful.

Hoo-hoo-hooo!

When Tigger feels **silly** and giggly,
he bounces like a ball!

Shh. . . .

Sometimes Piglet feels **shy**
when his friends are being noisy.

Oh no!

Roo gets scared when he sees
the shadows on his bedroom wall.

Harumph!

Rabbit gets grumpy when he sees that
someone has been in his garden.

Oh dear.

Eeyore is gloomy—because
that's just the way he is.

"Hmm?"

Owl is puzzled when he finishes his long, long story and sees that Pooh has fallen asleep.

Hooray!

Pooh feels excited when he finds a fresh batch of honey.

Best of all,

the friends in the Hundred-Acre Wood
feel *loved* by Christopher Robin.

Pooh's Day

Wake-Up Time

As soon as the sunshine
  says hello,
Pooh Bear makes his bed.
He wiggles his nose
and touches his toes,
and sings little songs in
  his head.

Playtime

In the middle of the morning
Pooh goes out to play.
He has a swing,
pretends he's king,
and looks forward to his day.

Lunchtime

Every single day at noon
Pooh Bear eats his honey.
Sometimes he slurps,
and then he burps.
He always thinks that's funny!

Craft Time

Some days after eating lunch,
Pooh has a craft to start.
He paints a flower
for a happy hour.
It's fun to make art.

Nap Time

Every sleepy afternoon
Pooh Bear takes a nap.
He dreams of things
with whistles and wings
that go "rap-a-tap-tap, a-tap-tap."

Dinnertime

While the sun is still awake,
Pooh sits down to eat.
He says a blessing
about honey dressing
and a world so sunny and sweet.

Story Time

Just before the sun disappears
Pooh turns on the light.
He looks at books
about princes and crooks
and things that go bump
in the night.

Bath Time

Every night when it gets dark
Pooh climbs into the tub.
He cleans his ears
so he can hear
and sings,
"Rub-dub-rub-dub-rub-dub."

Bedtime

When the sky is full of stars
Pooh Bear goes to sleep.
He closes his eyes
and wonders why
his head is full of sheep!

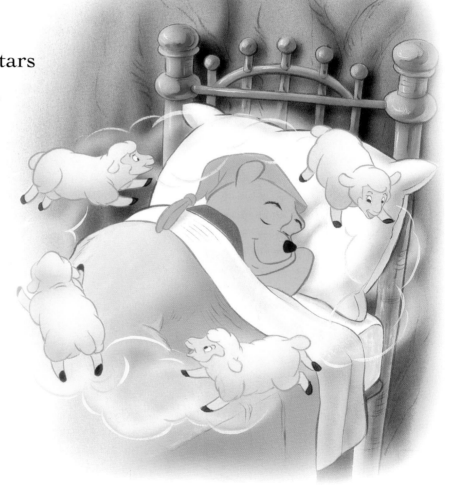

Pooh
Gets Stuck

"Oh bother," said Pooh. "My tummy is very rumbly, but my honey is all gone."

Pooh Bear set off to visit his good friend Rabbit.
Rabbit always had honey at his house.

"You're just in time for lunch," said Rabbit.

Pooh sat down at the table and ate . . .

and ate . . .

and ate more.

"Thank you for the honey," Pooh said at last in a rather sticky voice.

But as he tried to leave, Pooh's big, round tummy got in the way.

No matter how much Rabbit pushed, poked, and shoved, Pooh didn't budge. "I must find Christopher Robin," cried Rabbit as he ran out the back door.

"Silly old bear," said Christopher Robin. He and
Rabbit tugged and pulled, but Pooh stayed stuck.

"There's only one thing to do," said Christopher Robin. "We must wait for you to get thin again." So they waited.

When Eeyore saw what had happened, he said, "This could take days. Or weeks . . . or maybe even months."

"Oh bother," said Pooh. Rabbit agreed.

That night Gopher paid a hungry Pooh a visit. "Time for my midnight snack," said Gopher. "Would you like a taste, Pooh?"

Rabbit showed up just in time. "No!" he cried. "Not one drop of honey for Pooh." Then he put up a sign that read:

DO NOT FEED THE BEAR.

Time passed, but Pooh stayed stuck. Then one day, it happened. Pooh moved, but just a little bit.

Pooh's friends gathered around to help Pooh get unstuck. They pushed and pulled, and pushed a little more. . . .

Pop! Pooh flew out of
Rabbit's doorway and crashed
into a hollow tree. "Stuck
again," Eeyore said.

"Don't worry," Christopher
Robin called to Pooh. "We'll
get you right out of that tree."

Pooh was in no hurry. There was honey above him, below him, and all around him. "Take your time, Christopher Robin," Pooh shouted. "Take your time!"

Bedtime
Hummables

The Sleepover

Poor Piglet couldn't sleep,
so Pooh began to sing a sleeping hum:

I'm tucked in bed all snuggledy tight,
where things are always cuddledy right.
Snoozle-tea-pie, snoozle-tea-pie.

Sweet dreams will come to me tonight,
and soon will come the morning light.
Snoozle-tea-pie, snoozle-tea-pie.

"Want to hum along this time, Piglet?"
asked Pooh. "Piglet?"
But Piglet was fast asleep.

Bath Time

Splish, **splash.**
Scrub, scrub,
and rub-a-dub-dub—
Pooh Bear and Piglet
are in the bathtub.

Knock, knock.
Come in,
and rub-a-dub-dub—
Eeyore and Rabbit climb into the tub.

Knock, knock.
Come in,
and rub-a-dub-dub—
Kanga and Roo hop into the tub.

Knock, knock.
Come in,
and rub-a-dub-dub—
Tigger then bounces into the tub.

Pooh, Piglet, and Eeyore,
Rabbit, Kanga, and Roo—
plus Tigger, of course—
that makes quite a few.

Too many bathers,
and not enough tub.
No room for water
or rub-a-dub-dub!

Story Time

I've brushed my teeth.
I've washed my face.
I've put my pj's on.

I've climbed in bed,
laid down my head,
let out a great big yaw

I'm ready now
for story time—
where will we
go tonight?

To Make-believe
and back again—
you always tell it
right.

Sweet Dreams

Pj's and nightcap—
I'm ready for bed.
I pull up the sheets,
then lay down my head.

Soon I'm fast asleep.
I dream of yummy honey.
But when I awake,
something looks funny.

My honey is gone!
Oh dear me, oh my.
Who could have done this
while I slept nearby?

Bouncing at Bedtime

When Roos and Poohs are startin'
to snooze, a Tigger's night has just begun.

Tiggers bounce and pounce at bedtime
'cause we think it's fun-fun-fun!

Bouncing up and bouncing down,
my bed is a big trampoline.

A flip, a twist, a somersault—
I'm the best you've ever seen!

Bouncing high and bouncing low,
it's a glorious thing to do.

I think I'll spend all night bouncing
'cause I'm a Tigger, that's who!

In the Dark

Heffa-heffa-heffa-lump.
Scritchy-scratchy-scritch.
What makes that sound?
What makes that noise?
Could it have an itch?

Thumpa-wumpa-thumpa-wump.
Squeaky-squawky-squeak.
What makes that sound?
What makes that noise?
Dare I even peek?

The lights go on.
I look around,
and much to my surprise:
that heffalump's a pile of clothes—
no monster in disguise!

A Lullaby

Good night my baby,
my sweet kangaroo.
You're safe in my pocket—
and I'm here with you.
Soon you'll be big
and hop off on your own.
I'll be so proud
to see how you've grown.
But right now, my baby,
my sweet kangaroo,
you're safe in my pocket—
and I'm here with you.

Sweet Dreams, Baby